W9-BYI-216

Fighting Fires

by Susan Kuklin

FD 117 NY

117

Bradbury Press   New York

Maxwell Macmillan Canada   Toronto
Maxwell Macmillan International
New York   Oxford   Singapore   Sydney

The author would like to thank Fire Commissioner Carlos M. Rivera;
Battalion Chief Richard E. McGuire; the New York City Fire
Museum; Marilyn Bernard; Ladder Companies 12, 117, and 176;
Engine Companies 3 and 330; the fire fighters from the Division of
Training; and Domino, the firehouse dog of Ladder Company 43 and
Engine Company 53.

Bradbury Press, Macmillan Publishing Company, 866 Third Avenue, New York, NY 10022
Maxwell Macmillan Canada, Inc., 1200 Eglinton Avenue East, Suite 200, Don Mills, Ontario M3C 3N1
Macmillan Publishing Company is part of the Maxwell Communication Group of Companies.

First edition
Printed and bound in Singapore
10 9 8 7 6 5 4 3 2 1
The text of this book is set in 14 point Century Expanded.

LIBRARY OF CONGRESS CATALOGING-IN-PUBLICATION DATA

Kuklin, Susan.
Fighting fires / by Susan Kuklin. — 1st ed.
p.   cm.
Summary: Text and photographs present the vehicles, equipment, and
procedures used by fire fighters.
ISBN 0-02-751238-X
1. Fire fighters—Juvenile literature.   2. Fire extinction—
Juvenile literature.   [1. Fire fighters.   2. Fire extinction.]
I. Title.
TH9148.K85   1993
628.9′25—dc20   92-38678

To the fire fighters who have given their lives
in order to protect ours

CLANG! CLANG! CLANG! The fire truck pulls out from the station. Behind it will come the fire engine, also called the **pumper**. The truck and the pumper always travel together. Each has a special job to do. In fire fighters' language, these vehicles are both called **rigs**.

The officer of each rig sits in the cab next to the driver. He is in charge of the safety of the crew. He uses a radio, called a **Handie-Talkie**, and a computer to relay information to other rigs. Four or five other fire fighters ride in the cabin with lots of equipment.

Dalmatians are fire departments' unofficial mascots, or good-luck charms. Dalmatians ran with the horses that pulled the early fire engines. They guarded the horses from rats and robbers while the fire fighters were in the burning building.

Domino rides with his company every chance he gets.

Fire fighters wear high rubber boots and **turnout** coats to protect themselves as they work. Their coats have big yellow stripes that glow in the dark. They wear thick gloves and leather helmets to shield their hands and heads from the flames.

But that's not all. On their backs, fire fighters carry tall, skinny air tanks attached to masks, which they wear to protect themselves from the smoke. It all may look spooky, but the masks keep them safe.

Some fire fighters like to keep their ears uncovered. They listen for sounds when the smoke is too thick to see through. You might say they look with their ears.

The fire fighters who work on the fire truck sometimes call themselves **truckies**. The driver, known as the **chauffeur,** is responsible for the truck. He makes sure that the **tormentors** are down—they lift the entire truck off the ground. This keeps the truck steady when its ladder goes way up.

The chauffeur operates the tall ladder from a pedestal while two fire fighters ride in the bucket. They have special names, too: the **roof man** and the **outside vent man**. All fire fighters are nicknamed **men** because in earlier days only men had these jobs.

UP they go....

UP...

UP...

The truckies have two main jobs: to rescue people and to control the direction of the fire. While truckies closer to the ground search for people, the roof man uses a saw to cut a hole in the roof. This sends the smoke and flames up and out. Later, when the **pumper crew** is inside the building, the outside vent man will open doors and break windows. This gives the smoke and heat a place to go while the pumper crew is extinguishing the fire.

Nearer to the ground, other truckies use smaller ladders to search for people.

Meanwhile, the fire fighters from the pumper are hard at work. The pumper's driver, who also is called a chauffeur, uses a big hose to connect the front of the engine to a fire hydrant. Then he opens the hydrant to allow water to flow into the pumper.

You have to be very strong to work on the pumper. In addition to the air tanks, fire fighters must carry heavy hoses called **lines**, which are stored on the pumper. The lines are each fifty feet long, and they can all connect to one another.

Before the water is pumped to the fire, the officer from the truck goes into the building to make sure everyone has been rescued by the truckies. The officer finds exactly where the fire is. He relays the information to the pumper officer, who decides how many lines are needed to reach it. The pumper officer tells the crew where to stretch the lines.

Three fire fighters are needed to stretch the heavy line. Two people hold the line and one feeds it to them. The first person is called the **nozzle man** because he or she controls the nozzle. In this company, Zaida is the nozzle man.

The fire chief arrives at the fire in his own special car. He is the boss of both rigs. He uses a Handie-Talkie to tell the officers where to go and what needs to be done. You always know who the fire chief is because he wears a white helmet.

When the fire chief sees that all the preparations have been made, he directs the fire fighters from both rigs to continue on to the next phase of fighting the fire.

The truckies chop at walls and ceilings with axes and crowbars to get to the fire.

The pumper crew pulls the line into the building.

The officer of the pumper uses a Handie-Talkie to tell the chauffeur to turn on the water.

WHOOOOOSH! Water shoots out of the line, and the outside vent man gets to work.

It may look messy, but everyone knows exactly what to do.

Holding on to the heavy line with water blasting out is very hard. Even the strongest fire fighter needs a rest after a few minutes. The other fire fighters help control the line. When the nozzle man needs a break, she moves to the back position, and everyone else moves up.

At the pumper, the chauffeur works the dials of the pump to make sure the water is coming out at the right pressure.

If the fire's a big one, the chief calls in more rigs. Several rigs can hook their lines to the first pumper, to shoot water outside as well as inside.

Once the fire is out, everything must be cleaned up and put back into the rigs. The hydrant is closed and the lines are disconnected. Fire fighters lift the lines over their shoulders to drain the extra water. Everyone pitches in. All their tools are put back in the right place so that they will be ready for the next fire.

Fire fighters do lots of jobs. They can put out car fires with big fire extinguishers. They can rescue people who are stuck in high buildings or are trapped in cars. To be prepared, fire fighters practice saving each other, just so they never forget how.

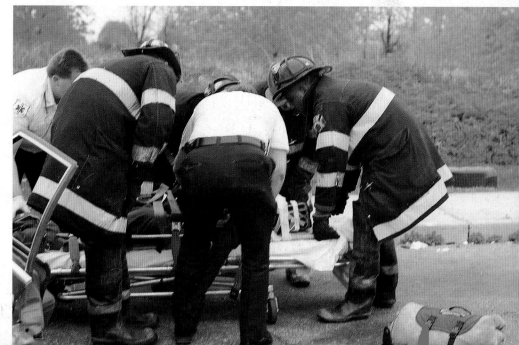

Rigs come in different shapes and sizes. A **tiller rig** is used to get around narrow streets. When the outside vent man steers the back part, he or she is called the **tiller man.**

Fire fighters sometimes give their rigs special names. This truck company calls its rig the Tin House Truck because their old firehouse had a tin roof.

Fat or skinny, old or new, the rig is specially cared for by the crew so that it will always be ready to get the job done.

For their bravery, fire fighters are often honored. The mayor comes to give them their medals at a special ceremony.

Fire fighters are proud of their jobs. They are really tired after a fire, but it is a good kind of tired. They say it's a good feeling to know that they helped save someone's life.

FIRE PREVENTION:

- Practice a safe fire-escape plan with your family.
- NEVER, EVER play with matches or fire.
- Take school fire drills seriously.
- Keep smoke detectors near every sleeping area.

IF THERE'S A FIRE:

- Never hide under beds or in closets.
- Get out fast.
- Never go back for anything.
- Call the fire department from a neighbor's house.
- If your clothes catch fire: STOP, DROP, ROLL.
- If there's smoke, drop to the floor and crawl toward a door or window. When you get to a door, if it feels HOT, crawl to a window to get some air. Shout to fire fighters to tell them where you are. If the door feels COLD, open with care, stay low, and go.
- Never fear fire fighters. They're your friends.

is based on guidelines generously provided by the New York City Fire Museum.